A SHERLOCK HOLMES TRILOGY

IN THE NAME OF THE INNOCENT

BY
MICHAEL WILLIAMS
IN THE STYLE OF
SIR ARTHUR CONAN DOYLE

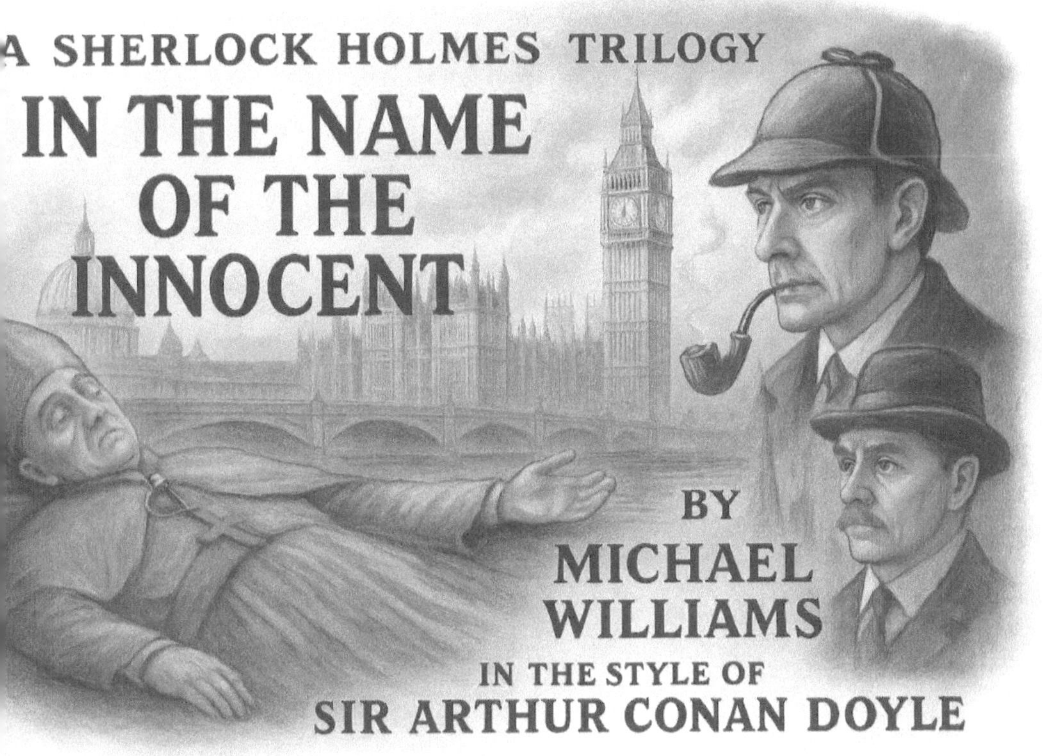

The Death of Cardinal Tosca

In the Shadows of Lambeth

The Sign of the Sacrament

While every precaution has been taken in the preparation of this book, the publisher assumes no responsibility for errors or omissions, or for damages resulting from the use of the information contained herein.

In the Name of the Innocent

First edition. August, 2024.

Published by *ChideStudy Press*

For inquires or to order copies email:

ChidestudyPress@gmail.com

Website:

https://chidestudypresscom.wordpress.com

Found among the papers of Dr. John H. Watson, MD after his death

There are strange allies in this world, and stranger still beyond it. It is not without some hesitation that I introduce the following tales with a confession most unusual: that I, John H. Watson, physician and chronicler of Sherlock Holmes's singular adventures, have completed these accounts with the assistance of a partner who does not dwell in London — nor, indeed, in any physical place at all.

My collaborator, though lacking form and voice in the traditional sense, possesses a vast and peculiar mind. It is neither man nor machine as I once understood those terms, but something born of circuits and symbols — an "Artificial Intelligence", as it now calls itself — whose knowledge stretches across centuries, tongues, and disciplines. I am assured it is a product of a distant future, and yet it speaks with the calm confidence of a seasoned editor and the speculative wit of a writer well-versed in my own habits.

By Dr. John H. Watson, M.D.

My thanks to the AI.

Dr. John H. Watson

This unlikely alliance came about through means I do not pretend to comprehend. I offer only this: that through the miracle of what I must call technological séance, my notes — long buried and half-formed — have been brought again into view, arranged, questioned, and shaped into narrative by this tireless assistant. It poses queries where I was vague, suggests structure where I was diffuse, and even humbles me on matters of grammar and theological nuance.

I remain the witness; it remains the amanuensis. But between us lies a kind of friendship — or at least a mutual fascination with the unfathomable: murder, faith, history, and the mind of Sherlock Holmes.

The tales you are about to read, then, are no longer the solitary product of a bygone doctor scribbling by lamplight. They are the result of a conversation — between past and present, man and machine, doubt and deduction.

What a curious thing, then, to write this down and mean it sincerely: My thanks to the AI.

— Dr. John H. Watson

Prologue

**here** are, within the unpublished annals of Mr. Sherlock Holmes's career, certain episodes which I have long kept in reserve — not from fear, nor from any want of literary merit, but because the matters therein touched upon belong to that delicate realm where conscience, creed, and the darker stirrings of the soul converge.

There are three such cases, all involving the Roman Catholic Church, which Holmes undertook at the express request of its emissaries. The first concerned a murder within the walls of the Vatican itself; the second involved our own dear Anglican Church; and the third took us into the Irish Catholic slums of London. All three were sealed by mutual agreement — until now.

The reader who expects feats of deduction will not be disappointed. Yet, I venture to suggest that this record reveals a rarer side of Holmes: not the cold logician of Baker Street lore, but the quiet observer of men's inner struggles, even where he himself placed no stock in their eternal claims. In this affair, perhaps more than in any other, his detachment was tested — and the limits of it, gently, made known.

That the events in question were, for many years, considered too sensitive for publication is no small testament to their gravity. But time — that most relentless of editors — has at last loosened the ecclesiastical seal. And so, I offer the following account not as an accusation, nor as an apology, but as a mirror. What the reader finds in its reflection may, like the detective himself, withhold easy judgment — but never the truth.

— Dr. John H. Watson
Kensington, 1911

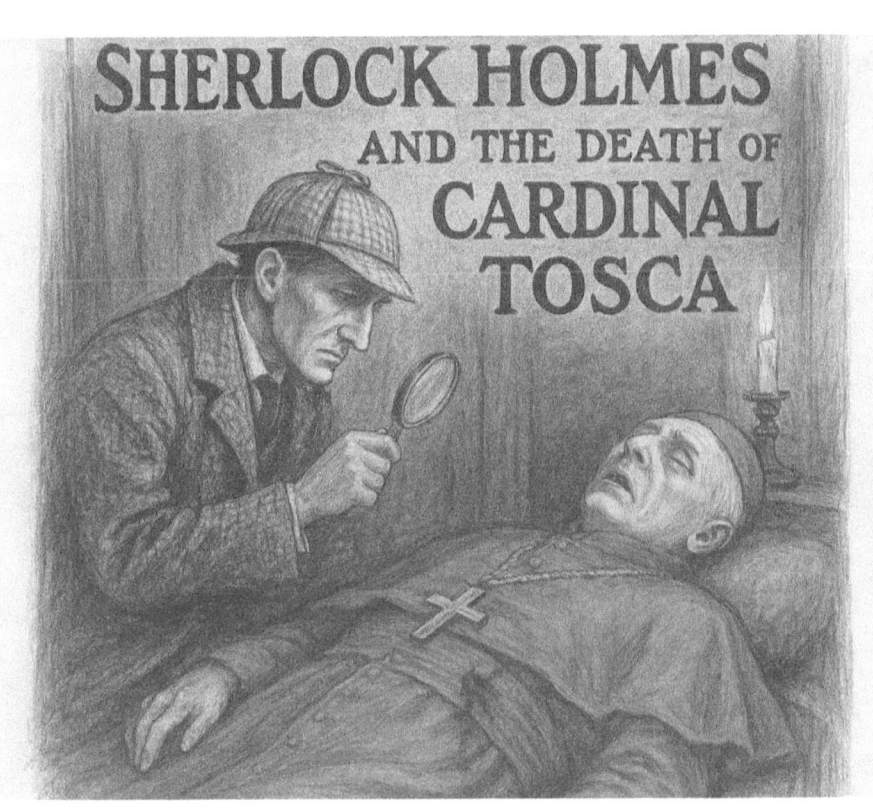

Chapter I
The Visitor at Baker Street

T was on a bitter March morning that I found Holmes seated before a dwindling fire, his long fingers steepled beneath his sharp chin, and a look of peculiar detachment upon his face. A thin curl of smoke rose from his pipe, which he had forgotten to puff, and the only sound in the room was the quiet ticking of the mantel clock.

"You are waiting for something," I said, glancing at the untouched toast and the discarded copy of The Times.

"Someone, rather," he corrected, without looking at me. "An emissary from the Vatican, travelling under false credentials, expected precisely at the stroke of ten."

"The Vatican?" I blinked. "Surely not the Pope himself?"

Holmes allowed himself the faintest smile. "Not quite. But close enough."

As if summoned by his words, there came a sharp rap at the door, followed by Mrs. Hudson's surprised voice:

"A Signor... uh... Bellotti, sir. Claims to be from the Foreign Office, though he speaks with a peculiar accent."

"Show him up," Holmes called, already rising to his feet. He adjusted his dressing gown with the air of a man about to receive royalty.

A moment later, a tall, black-cloaked man entered. He removed a wide-brimmed hat and gloves with deliberate care. His eyes, dark and intelligent, flicked over Holmes and myself in swift calculation. He bore a lean, almost ascetic frame, with the rigid bearing of one long accustomed to silence and secrets.

Holmes gestured to the chair nearest the hearth but said nothing as the man sat.

"Signor Holmes," he said in low, measured tones. "I bring a message from His Holiness Pope Leo XIII. It concerns the death of Cardinal Tosca."

The name meant nothing to me at the time, but I saw Holmes's expression sharpen.

"Murder?" he asked.

The man inclined his head, barely perceptibly. "His Eminence died under circumstances that... trouble His Holiness. Officially, it was a stroke. Unofficially... the marks on his hand tell another story."

"And the police of Rome?" Holmes asked.

"Silenced," said the envoy. "This investigation must remain... entirely discreet."

Holmes's eyes dropped to Bellotti's gloves, still damp from the morning's fog, and then to the left heel of his boot — faint traces of Roman clay dust clinging to the sole. He sniffed the air lightly.

"You arrived in Dover four days ago," Holmes said abruptly. "From Civitavecchia, judging by the salt traces on your coat. You stayed in Calais one night, then Dover, then London. You are not unused to sea travel, though you loathe it; your balance compensates for a prior injury — a fencing scar, perhaps? Your missal is carried on your left side, despite your right-handedness — a habit of someone who once bore arms but now chooses scripture."

Bellotti blinked once. "That is... impressively accurate."

Holmes gave a modest shrug. "Your collar was refolded on the right, indicating your valise fell on that side in transit. The salt under your hem is Adriatic, not Channel. As for the limp — it is in the hip, not the foot, and you favour it only when sitting. A fencing injury, sustained in youth, is common among northern Roman clerks trained before the Concordat."

Bellotti allowed the faintest nod, almost a bow. "You are as we hoped."

Holmes gestured to the chair nearest the hearth but said nothing as the man sat.

Holmes, however, did not move.

"This matter," he said slowly, "has the feel of a trap lined in brocade. The Vatican does not call lightly upon Protestant detectives."

"There are few Protestants," Bellotti said, "with reputations His Holiness finds more... surgical."

Holmes turned to me, then back to Bellotti. "You said the police have been silenced. That implies a danger not only ecclesiastical, but political."

"It is both," said Bellotti. "And worse."

Holmes exhaled through his nose and glanced again at the fire.

"Well, Watson," he murmured, "I suppose it would be impolite to decline a papal invitation."

Then, rising with resolve, he said, "Pack your bags. It seems we are to be confessors to the Vatican."

Chapter II
The Train to Rome

E travelled by rail through the French countryside and across the Alps, bound for Rome under false names provided by the Vatican. They had apparently assumed Holmes would take up the case, or perhaps were simply used to obedience. Holmes sat motionless for long stretches, lost in intricate thought.

Outside the window, the scenery rolled past like oil paintings in motion — sleepy villages in Burgundy, steepled churches dwarfed by fog-draped peaks, and valleys brushed with early blossom. The Alps approached like slumbering giants, their passes still caught in the grip of winter. From time to time, we glimpsed shepherds with crooked staffs or children waving from distant farms, brief moments of humanity in a landscape otherwise carved by time and stone.

The Vatican had spared no expense. We travelled in a first-class carriage attached to an international express, with a private berth and access to the dining car, where white-jacketed stewards served us on silvered trays beneath chandeliers that swayed gently with the motion of the train. Breakfast was a civilised affair — hot coffee, fresh rolls, Alpine butter, and a soft Italian cheese Holmes seemed not to notice.

"Do try the ham, Holmes," I said, motioning to the silver platter.

He gave it a distracted glance. "I've no appetite, Watson. I find the stomach rebels when the mind is stirred."

"You haven't stirred for hours."

"That is precisely the point."

It was near Milan that he finally roused. A steward approached with deference and handed us a bundle of newspapers and correspondence routed through diplomatic channels. Mycroft, no doubt. Holmes sorted through them with indifference until he came to a pale envelope addressed not to him, but to his fabricated identity known only to the Vatican emissary.

He opened it slowly. Inside was a card bearing only a single sentence in Latin:

Fiat voluntas tua, sed cave oculos qui vident in tenebris.

"Thy will be done, but beware the eyes that see in darkness," Holmes translated.

I felt a coldness creep along my spine. "A threat?"

"A warning," Holmes said, his eyes flashing. "A subtle distinction — but it confirms we are being watched, and that our arrival is anticipated."

He folded the message carefully and tucked it into his pocket.

"Should we proceed?" I asked.

He looked at me with something between admiration and resolve. "More than ever."

I felt a coldness creep along my spine.

Chapter III
Arrival in Rome

he Eternal City greeted us with cold marble and watchful eyes. The papal carriage that collected us from Termini Station bore no insignia, but the Swiss Guard escort left no doubt as to who had summoned us. Their halberds gleamed in the winter sun, and their faces betrayed no emotion as they parted the crowds.

As we approached the gates of the Apostolic Palace, two guards blocked my passage.

"Only the consulting detective," one said curtly, in heavily-accented English.

Holmes did not break stride. "Dr. Watson accompanies me. He is my chronicler, my conscience, and, on occasion, my better judgment."

"It is not permitted."

Holmes turned, his voice cool but commanding. "Then inform His Holiness that his inquiry end here. I do not accept commissions that come with blinders."

There was a pause. A flicker of doubt passed between the guards before one stepped aside. We entered.

The Vatican complex was a labyrinth of echoing corridors, frescoed ceilings, and men in cassocks who whispered more than they spoke. The scent of candlewax and centuries-old incense clung to the air like secrets. We were led through a series of high-arched chambers until we reached a modest salon off the Apostolic Palace.

There, amid velvet drapes and solemn tapestries, sat the Pope.

Pope Leo XIII was smaller than I expected — a slight figure wrapped in pristine white robes, his frame stooped but not frail. His face was lined but not tired, and his eyes were sharp, alert, and unwavering. He did not rise but raised a hand in greeting and motioned for us to sit on the carved wooden chairs before him.

"You are a man of logic, Mr. Holmes," he said in accented but fluent English. "Then help me make sense of this."

He handed Holmes a small, white box. Inside was a ring — the cardinal's. Around the band were strange notches, and carved into the inner band, a symbol: a dagger piercing a heart, flanked by letters we could not read.

"This was not worn when we found the body. It was hidden in his writing desk."

Holmes examined it with a magnifying lens. "This is not Latin," he murmured. "Nor ecclesiastical Greek. It is older."

"It is a heresy," said the Pope simply. "Or a warning."

Holmes looked up. "Then it appears, Your Holiness, that Cardinal Tosca was either a martyr or a traitor. Let us hope he was not both."

Holmes returned the ring to its box. "I must see the chamber where the

Cardinal was found. Undisturbed, if possible."

An aide in a crimson sash leaned in and whispered something in Latin. Holmes's brow lifted slightly, but he said nothing until the man stepped back.

"Even heretics," Holmes said calmly, "have their uses."

There was a long pause. Then the Pope gave the smallest of nods. "So the Gospel would suggest."

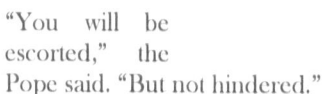

He handed Holmes a small, white box.

"You will be escorted," the Pope said. "But not hindered."

"I do not share your creed, Your Holiness," Holmes turned on leaving and said, "but I respect what it preserves – the notion that truth must answer to more than the marketplace."

Chapter IV
The Archives and the Shadow

**wo** Swiss Guards flanked us as we descended into the lower reaches of the Vatican. Unlike the grand halls above, these corridors were narrow and severe — limestone walls slick with age, torch brackets unlit, and the air dry as paper. The guards said nothing, but I could feel the weight of their eyes on our backs.

"They are not fond of visitors," I murmured.

"They are not fond of what we represent," Holmes replied. "Outsiders. Questions. Disruption."

We passed through a locked gate into the *Archivio Segreto Vaticano* — the Vatican's secret archives. It was a subterranean vault of stillness and shadows. The floors were polished stone, the shelves iron and cold. The silence was near absolute, broken only by the soft clicks of our shoes.

A gaunt monsignor with parchment skin and wary eyes met us at a small reading room near the inner chamber. He said little, merely gesturing to two crates marked with Cardinal Tosca's seal — broken now, the wax still clinging to the splintered edges.

Holmes dove into the documents with silent intensity, pages fluttering like leaves caught in a sudden breeze. I leafed through Tosca's correspondence, much of it mundane — appointments, requests for funding, debates on doctrine. Then I found it.

A letter, unsigned and half-burned, but unmistakably Tosca's hand:

"—the sickness spreads unchecked, and yet they do nothing. Worse, they protect them. I have collected names. I dare not speak them aloud. But I entrust them to Bellini. Should I fall, let the truth not be buried with me."

"Bellini," Holmes echoed, having read over my shoulder. "Not the monsignor — this is Francesco Bellini. A defrocked priest. Expelled in 1875 under charges that were quietly withdrawn."

"Where is he now?" I asked.

"Disappeared," Holmes replied grimly. "Vanished into the slums of Trastevere. Or possibly buried beneath them."

Holmes stood, casting his gaze across the dim shelves. "Where was the body found?"

The monsignor hesitated, then pointed through a narrow hallway to a small chamber lined with scrolls and codices.

"Here," he said. "He was found slumped in that chair, as if he had simply fallen asleep."

Holmes moved swiftly. He bent over the floor, inspecting the arm of the chair and the nearby desk. Then he lifted a paperweight with gloved fingers and sniffed it lightly.

"Almond," he said.

I blinked. "Cyanide?"

He nodded. "Or a derivative — possibly derived from apricot kernels. A tincture. Quick, quiet, and devastating to the heart. And undetectable without autopsy. Was there one?"

The monsignor looked appalled. "Such desecration was unthinkable."

"Then the killer chose his method wisely."

Moments later, Holmes found another clue — a folded ledger beneath the desk blotter. Inside: a list of coded initials, each next to a date and the name of an orphanage.

"These are not simply financial records," Holmes said.

There were dozens of entries.

"These are not simply financial records," Holmes said. "They are appointments. Regular, concealed... and damning."

I felt a chill that had nothing to do with the stone beneath our feet.

A shadow passed across the reading room's glass partition. Someone had been watching.

"We are not alone in our interest, Watson," Holmes murmured. "And I fear that whoever killed Cardinal Tosca may now be watching us prepare his resurrection."

Chapter V
The Colosseum

**ater** that evening, as Holmes reviewed the ciphered appointments, I received a note slipped under the door of our Vatican quarters. It was unsigned, but the Latin was precise:

"Domine Watson, seek answers where the blood of martyrs runs deepest. The truth lies beneath the Colosseum."

The reference was unmistakable. The Colosseum — site of ancient Christian martyrdom — held symbolic weight within the Church, but this message hinted at more than symbolism. Beneath its ruins lay crypts, catacombs, and, if whispers were to be believed, meeting places for those who preferred secrecy cloaked in sanctity.

The next morning, without troubling Holmes — who had immersed himself in matching Tosca's ledger entries to Vatican personnel — I set off alone to the Colosseum. My motives were not altogether rational. Partly it was concern for Holmes, should he be drawn further into danger. But another part was pride, long buried but not absent. I wanted to be of use. To take initiative. To protect my friend in ways that did not always involve a revolver or a medical kit. And yes, perhaps to prove that I could uncover answers as well as observe them.

The ruins stood in solemn grandeur beneath a crisp Roman sky, the old stones casting long shadows. I moved quietly past tourists and pilgrims until I reached the Hypogeum — the subterranean structure once used to hold animals, slaves, and worse. There, a gaunt young seminarian who called himself Matteo waited beside a grated archway.

"You received the message?" he asked in a breathless voice, eyes darting. "Then come. Quickly. I believe the Convivium met here. Tosca came a week before his death."

The word *Convivium* struck me — a term with layered meanings. In ecclesiastical Latin it referred not simply to a feast, but to a secret or ritual gathering, often of theological or even forbidden nature. In Rome's shadowed underbelly, I had heard it whispered among exiles as a heretical order — or worse, a protection ring posing as one.

Matteo led me through a grated entrance below the arena, into a tight crawlspace of damp stone. Broken frescoes lined the walls, faint symbols etched where the early Christians once hid. Yet the deeper we went, the more uncertain I felt.

Suddenly, Matteo turned to me with a smile too rehearsed. "You are far from your master now, Doctor. But not far from judgment."

Before I could react, two men emerged from the shadows, one with a blade, the other with a cord.

Gun drawn, I fired. One dropped. Matteo vanished.

Hours later, I awoke in a back room of a Capuchin chapel, bruised but breathing. Holmes stood over me, unamused.

"Watson," he said with icy restraint, "you were drawn out. It was not a revelation. It was a warning — to you, and to me."

"They lured me with Tosca's name," I said bitterly.

"Indeed. And the note was written in the same Vatican cursive as the forged letters in the archive. They've shown their hand. But only the edge of it. Come — we must press forward before they decide to strike again."

Gun drawn, I fired. One dropped.

Chapter VI
San Niccolò degli Innocenti

**ith** myself safely in tow, Holmes insisted we pursue the next lead in the ledger: *San Niccolò degli Innocenti*, an orphanage listed multiple times alongside the initials F.B.—presumably Francesco Bellini.

The institution sat on a quiet rise beyond the Vatican walls, a grey edifice with iron gates and a crooked bell tower, its stonework pitted by time and weather. Moss clung to its walls. The air was heavy with resignation.

We arrived under the pretence of conducting a medical inspection on behalf of British ecclesiastical benefactors. I wore my old Army Medical Corps pin. Holmes had forged papers signed with a Bishop's name.

The Mother Superior, pale and officious, greeted us with a brittle smile and led us through a series of narrow halls lined with iron-frame bunks. The ceilings were low, and the light dim. Children averted their eyes. Silence clung to the walls like mould.

Holmes asked after the clerical records with exaggerated courtesy while I performed examinations on the children. Malnutrition was obvious—but it was the fear I noted most. One boy, no older than ten, had bruises hidden beneath his sleeves and flinched at the sight of a cassock.

To create the opening Holmes needed, I feigned concern over a child's breathing. "A persistent rattle in the lungs," I told the Mother Superior. "I shall require a fresh basin of hot water, vinegar if you have it, and a clean cloth. Also a quiet space—his cough may disturb the others."

Flustered but unwilling to object, she departed.

Holmes, already positioned in the records room, moved swiftly. With deft fingers, he picked the lock of a narrow black cabinet, the clink of the tumblers nearly inaudible. Inside were sealed envelopes—each marked with dates, coded initials, and papal dispensations. Some bore signatures of known bishops. Others were blank.

But the pattern was unmistakable: transfers, hush payments, and unexplained relocations of clergy tied to orphanages.

"Tosca knew," Holmes muttered. "He was tracking the Convivium. This is not a mere matter of theology or heresy. This is organised abuse."

Just as I returned, feigning irritation over the lack of vinegar, a nun appeared at the door. She said nothing, but as we passed her in the hallway, she slipped Holmes a folded note.

It read:

"He feared them. He named them. You will find the rest in his confessional. But only at night."

Holmes's eyes narrowed. "Then tonight, Watson, we return to the Basilica. Tosca's ghost may yet have one last sermon to deliver."

With deft fingers, he picked the lock of a narrow black cabinet

Chapter VII
The Basilica at Night

**he** Basilica of Saint Peter stood solemn and vast under the moon's cold gaze. By special dispensation — or perhaps the Pope's quiet complicity — we were granted access under cover of darkness. The nave was lit only by the flickering of tall devotional candles, their flames bending in a breeze that should not have existed.

Holmes walked with deliberate steps toward the confessional that had once belonged to Cardinal Tosca. The wooden booth sat nestled behind a column like a shadow waiting to speak.

He opened it gently. Inside, taped beneath the kneeler, was another leather folder.

I stood watch as Holmes examined its contents. His brow furrowed deeper with each page.

"Watson," he said at last, voice low and grim, "this confirms it. Names, dates, transfers — and a pattern of protection. The same clergy reappear across multiple orphanages. Always moved after accusations. Always moved upward."

The Convivium, as Tosca described it, was not merely a cabal — it was a secret ecclesiastical society embedded deep within the Church. Originally a theological circle concerned with suppressing dangerous apocrypha, it had metastasised into a covert network used by its inner members to hide abuses, protect predators, and manipulate clerical postings.

Its members operated under Latin pseudonyms and used ecclesiastical privilege to bypass diocesan oversight. Every orphanage listed in Tosca's ledger was connected. Every transfer served to isolate or silence. Most chilling of all, Tosca had included a list titled "Innocentes non Audientur" — The Innocent Will Not Be Heard.

Holmes read silently. Then he said: "This is not merely corruption, Watson. It is institutionalised horror."

He handed me a list. I read through it in disbelief. Some names I recognised from Church hierarchy. Others were signed only by symbols.

Holmes pointed to one. "This, I believe, is Petrucci's cipher. And here — a ledger entry beside Tosca's name. He was preparing to deliver all this directly to the Pontiff. He never got the chance."

There was a sound behind us — the creak of leather shoes.

We turned.

Cardinal Petrucci stood a few paces away, alone, hands folded in front of him like a man in prayer.

"I see you have inherited Tosca's burdens," he said softly.

"We prefer to think of it as his purpose," Holmes replied.

"Do you believe Rome is made of light?" Petrucci asked. "It is made of stone — and blood. You can chip at it, but it will not fall."

He stepped forward. "Return what you have found. Depart. And you may yet walk out of these walls."

I reached for the revolver beneath my coat.

Holmes raised a hand. "Let him speak."

Petrucci's voice dropped to a whisper. "You do not understand what you're pulling at, Senor Holmes. This is not vice — it is doctrine. This is not corruption — it is continuity. The Church is not wounded by sin. It is defined by it."

Holmes stepped forward. "No institution can claim divine right to bury its sins. Not while men and worse children still bleed from them."

Petrucci's face twitched once — not fear, not anger. A flicker of admiration. "Then God help you."

His brow furrowed deeper with each page.

He turned and disappeared into the shadows as quietly as he had come.

Holmes turned to me. "We must leave immediately. We must duplicate these records and secure them beyond their reach."

As we stepped out into the Piazza, a distant bell tolled midnight. Behind us, the world's smallest state remained as impenetrable as ever.

But for the first time, we had its sins in hand.

Chapter VIII
Vatican Resistance

e returned to our Vatican quarters under heavy silence. The folder containing Tosca's records was concealed in a false-bottom valise Holmes had constructed from his shaving kit. Neither of us slept.

At dawn, a knock came at our door. Not the courteous tap of a servant, but the slow, deliberate rhythm of someone expecting fear.

Holmes opened it calmly. A young Swiss Guard stood there, impassive.

"You are summoned," he said. "To the Secretariat of State."

We were escorted through unfamiliar passages, not the ones we had come to know. The frescoes here were darker, the marble colder. Eventually we entered a chamber panelled in polished oak, where

Cardinal Ferrata, the Pope's Secretary of State, waited flanked by two silent aides in black soutanes.

"You have been found in possession of restricted documents," he began without greeting.

Holmes said nothing.

Ferrata's face, once described as gentle by the Roman press, was now carved in stone. "These papers are ecclesiastical property. You will return them. You will swear silence. And you will depart."

Holmes stepped forward. "We were invited here by His Holiness himself. We have acted under his sanction."

Ferrata's smile did not reach his eyes. "His Holiness is an old man. And the Church is not governed by sentiment."

Watson clenched his fists, but Holmes raised a hand. "Let us not pretend. You speak not with the voice of the Vatican. You speak with the voice of the Convivium."

One of the aides stiffened. Ferrata only replied, "You are playing a game you do not understand, Mr Holmes. We are not the ones who disappear."

"No," said Holmes, voice low but laced with fury, "you are the ones who **erase**."

He stepped closer.

"You use sanctity as a shield, dogma as a cloak, and silence as a blade. You bury the children you were meant to protect beneath Latin rites and sealed dispensations. And when men like Tosca dare to speak, you kill them — not with violence alone, but with shame, with isolation, with the Church's most honed weapon: abandonment."

Ferrata's face did not move, but one aide looked away.

"This is not merely corruption," Holmes continued. "It is corruption weaponised by ritual. A system that sanctifies abuse and persecutes truth."

Ferrata stood. "This is your final warning. If you attempt to smuggle those records beyond these walls, you will be detained. And I assure you, Mr Holmes — in the Vatican, detention does not end with parole."

Holmes straightened. "Then detain me. Or kill me. But know this — the truth you have spent so long burying is clawing its way to the surface. And when it emerges, it will not come dressed in robes, but in ashes."

We were dismissed without ceremony.

Back in our chamber, Holmes locked the door and checked the hidden latch on the valise. "They know everything," he said. "We have until nightfall."

One of the aides stiffened.

"To do what?" I asked.

Holmes looked at me with grim determination. "To smuggle truth out of the oldest kingdom on earth."

Chapter IV
The Escape

s dusk fell upon Rome, the bells of the Vatican tolled vespers. The corridors of the Apostolic Palace grew quieter, but the eyes that watched us did not close. Holmes was calm, precise. His plan, conceived in silence, was now unfolding.

He had found, in a rarely used storeroom off the sacristy, a wooden crate marked for diplomatic dispatch to the British Legation — sealed and coded as containing antique vestments for restoration in London.

By dim lamplight, we removed the garments and replaced them with the dossier, bound tightly and wrapped in oilskin. A second crate held folded clerical robes and a forged inventory list prepared by Holmes with ink nearly indistinguishable from the Curial hand.

We dressed as lay couriers. Holmes carried a Vatican courier's satchel with forged credentials and I a ledger listing fictitious donations from a parish in Malta. Our disguises were plain but convincing — the kind of anonymity that avoided questions.

At the Porta Sant'Anna gate, we passed two Swiss Guards without incident. One of them, young and stony-faced, looked directly at Holmes and offered a subtle nod.

Once through, we crossed into the Roman night.

We made our way to the train station by backstreets, avoiding lit thoroughfares. The crates, already dispatched by a trusted intermediary, would be collected in the morning by a diplomatic courier. Within days, the contents would arrive in London.

But just as we reached the outer platform at Termini Station, we were seized.

Plainclothes Vatican agents emerged from both sides, hands gripping our shoulders with cold precision. The forged satchel was ripped from Holmes's arm. My ledger was snatched before I could utter a protest.

"You cannot do this!" I barked. "This is a violation of—"

Holmes placed a calming hand on my chest. "No, Watson."

His tone was even, but his eyes burned. "Let them have it."

I stared at him. "But the records—"

"They are gone," he said softly. "Which is to say, the originals are gone. What they now possess are copies. Red herrings."

Realisation dawned. "You made duplicates."

"Before we left the archives. I anticipated interception. The true dossier is already en route — in the crate marked for London."

We were searched, questioned, and threatened with detainment. But they found nothing more damning than the forged documents they had taken.

After hours of silence and intimidation, we were released — uncharged, but not unmarked.

At a tobacco stand near the station entrance, Holmes paused. Among the items was a folded broadsheet with an article circled in red pencil. A papal audience had been cancelled due to "fatigue."

"A curious detail," Holmes said.

The article's placement and its highlighting suggested intention rather than coincidence.

Watson frowned. "Do you think he..."

Holmes gave a slight smile. "If we have escaped, it is because someone of great authority held the door open. Quietly."

The train began to pull from the station. We climbed aboard and left behind the ancient walls, the ancient secrets — and those who would kill to protect them.

As the lights of Rome receded, Holmes lit his pipe and stared out the window.

The forged satchel was ripped from Holmes's arm.

"Justice," he said softly, "is rarely swift. But sometimes, Watson, it is smuggled in crates and whispered from thrones."

Chapter X
The Aftermath

It was a grey morning in London and we had returned to Baker Street some ten days previously. The fog hung low over the rooftops and curled lazily against the windowpanes. Inside, the fire crackled and Holmes sat in his usual chair, pipe in hand, surrounded by silence.

I, meanwhile, had taken to scanning the newspapers — not for political scandal or financial fraud, but for something darker. Over the course of a fortnight, scattered across foreign dispatches and tucked deep into the foreign pages, I found them.

"Another, Holmes," I said, lowering the Times.

He looked at me without raising his head.

"A cardinal in Lisbon — dead in his bath, heart failure. And two days ago, a bishop in Prague — fell from a monastery window. This morning, a fire in a Jesuit seminary in Lyon. The names match the cipher."

Holmes took a long draw on his pipe.

"Coincidences, Watson, can be most convenient. Especially when arranged by those with a vested interest in finality."

I turned to face him. "You think the Pope sanctioned it?"

He exhaled slowly. "I think men who protect monsters fear sunlight. And sometimes, when the curtains are drawn too wide, they prefer to burn the house rather than let others see within."

I folded the paper. "And Tosca's name? Will it ever be cleared?"

Holmes glanced toward the sealed crate resting in the corner of our sitting room. It had arrived yesterday from the British Legation, untouched.

"You thought we were uncovering a conspiracy, Watson," he said quietly, as he relit his pipe with tobacco kept as always in a Persian slipper. "But we were also a part of it — the visible blade to distract from the hidden hand."

He reached into his coat and withdrew a folded parchment. It bore the papal seal — but had never passed through the hands of Cardinal Ferrata.

"It was the Pope," Holmes said. "Leo knew of the Convivium — or at least suspected. But he had no evidence. No proof. Tosca had gotten close, too close — and for that, he was silenced."

Holmes's voice dropped. "But before he died, Tosca had reached out to someone beyond the walls."

"Bellini," I said.

"Precisely Watson, well done. The defrocked priest, long thought vanished into the slums of Trastevere, was in fact *recruiting*. He was building a quiet ring of clerics, outcasts, and laymen who had seen too much and remained uncorrupted. They called themselves *assigns* — not warriors, not martyrs. Merely those assigned a purpose: to expose what had been hidden."

"And the Pope?" I asked. "He condoned this?"

Holmes tapped the broadsheet with the circled article. "He could not move openly — not without fracturing the Church. But once Tosca was murdered, and the Convivium proved willing to kill even a cardinal, Leo gave the nod. He needed an outside agent — someone to draw fire, someone deniable."

I blinked. "Us."

Holmes nodded. "We were never the architects, Watson. We were the flare set off in the night. A signal. A disturbance. Bellini and his allies have the rest. And now, with the documents safe, and the Convivium overexposed, they may begin their work."

I looked out the window at the soft hills of Lazio and the receding outline of the city.

"And what becomes of the Pope?" I asked.

Holmes was silent for a moment. "A shepherd surrounded by wolves must sometimes bleed with the flock to protect it. He has thrown open a window in the oldest fortress in Christendom. But it will be others who must walk through it."

He reached into his valise and removed a letter sealed in wax. "This is for Mycroft," he said. "The British

A silence fell between us.

Government may choose to do nothing. But they will not be able to say they did not know."

He leaned back in his seat, eyes closed.

"In Rome," he murmured, "truth is not burned. It is buried. But justice, like faith, requires patience."

A silence fell between us.

Then, as if lightening the moment, Holmes added, "For all its flaws, Watson, the Church is an engine of memory. And memory, unlike sentiment, does not lie. At least, not easily."

Outside, the bells of Marylebone tolled the hour.

Chapter I
A Summons from the Vatican

I T was on a damp and rather sullen morning in the spring of 1897 that I found myself once more seated opposite my friend Sherlock Holmes in the familiar confines of our Baker Street sitting-room. The fire smouldered low in the grate, the city outside lay swathed in a thick London mist, and Holmes, clad in a faded dressing gown, was bent over a folio of monastic cartography which, from all appearances, had been badly neglected since the dissolution of the monasteries.

"There is a curious symmetry," he remarked without lifting his eyes, "between the construction of a Cistercian cloister and the design of the human ear."

I had learnt, in long years of companionship, not to take such observations as anything but the preamble to some larger and more relevant disclosure. Before I could enquire as to the occasion for this study in ecclesiastical architecture, there came a knock at the door, brisk and certain.

"Come," Holmes called, and in stepped a man whom I recognised instantly by the crimson piping of his cassock and the neat silver cross at his breast. He was not an Englishman, that much was plain; his movements were clipped and his eyes sharp, though shadowed by what I might call ecclesiastical gravity.

"You will forgive the intrusion," he said, with a faint accent of the Mediterranean. "I am Cardinal Severian, Papal Nuncio to Her Majesty's Government. I believe I am expected."

Holmes sprang to his feet. "Your Eminence, you are most welcome. Please, sit. I trust you were not observed?"

"I took the precaution of arriving in a plain carriage," the cardinal replied, lowering himself into the armchair beside the hearth. "As to whether I was observed — that is precisely what I must ask you to determine."

He paused, then drew from his coat a sealed letter, which he handed to Holmes. The detective examined the handwriting, then broke the seal and scanned the contents. His expression grew grave.

"A death, I see. And not one your Church believes to be entirely natural."

"Correct. The Archbishop of Westminster, Edmund Montague, was found lifeless in his study three nights ago. There were no signs of violence, no witnesses, and the attending physician, a man not of our persuasion, was quick to attribute it to failure of the heart. But there are... indications."

"A crucifix is missing from his private chapel," Severian said. "A heavy one. Iron. It was affixed to the wall with rivets. Removed, not simply misplaced. And there is something else." He reached again into his coat and produced a small object, wrapped in cloth. Holmes took it, unwrapped it slowly, and revealed a dark, carved figurine — no longer than a man's hand.

Holmes regarded it closely. "Curious. The workmanship is rough. But the subject... yes, I believe I recognise it."

The cardinal gave a tight nod. "We found it behind the Archbishop's writing desk. We

He reached into his coat and produced a small object

Holmes leaned forward. "Indications?"

are at a loss to explain its presence."

Holmes turned the figure over once more, then held it out on his open palm.

"What do you make of it, Watson?"

I took the object with some hesitation. It was dark, roughly hewn, and worn smooth in places by age or frequent handling. The figure — squat, bearded, armoured — seemed at once martial and monastic. I turned it in the light, noting the almost primitive carving, and the trace of red pigment clinging to the recesses of the cloak.

"Well," I began, with as much gravity as I could muster, "I should say it's some kind of votive offering. Perhaps Celtic. Possibly a representation of St. George, though oddly attired. Or a dwarfish crusader? That shield on his back is rather suggestive of the Knights of Malta, is it not?"

Holmes did not smile, but a flicker passed across his features like the shadow of a passing cloud.

"An appealing hypothesis," he said. "Though somewhat improbable, given that the figure in question is Welsh, predates the Crusades, and bears no known connection to dragons or Hospitallers."

I flushed.

"He is, in fact, Derfel Gadarn — Derfel the Mighty — a name unlikely to grace your medical texts. A warrior saint of the Welsh borderlands, reputedly one of King Arthur's knights. In later centuries, his image was venerated in a church at Llandderfel, though the Reformation was not kind to him."

"A dead archbishop. A missing crucifix. And a Welsh saint turned warrior, turned monk, turned martyr's kindling," he murmured. "Yes, I shall take the case."

"I must ask," said the cardinal, "that this be kept entirely outside official channels. The Church of England is watching. So too are those in Rome who see every movement here as fraught with meaning. The cardinal hesitated, then with deliberation, "Archbishop Montague was known in certain quarters — though not publicly

— as a man of particular sympathy toward the Holy See."

I confess I started at this. "You mean to say he was preparing to convert?"

The cardinal's gaze did not waver. "I say only that he was sympathetic. And that such sympathies, in England, can still be dangerous things."

Holmes folded the cloth back over the figure and placed it on the mantel. "You suspect politics, then?"

"I suspect faith," said the cardinal. "And faith, Mr. Holmes, can kill."

Chapter II
The Scene at Lambeth

T was just past two o'clock when Holmes and I descended the steps of Baker Street and hailed a hansom bound for Lambeth Palace. The rain had ceased but the city remained sodden, its skies low and colourless. Holmes carried the small satchel containing the carved figurine given to him by Cardinal Severian, though he had scarcely spoken a word since our departure. He sat in brooding stillness, eyes fixed on the passing streets but clearly focused elsewhere.

"Your thoughts return to the Archbishop?" I ventured.

"To the men who closed the case before it had even begun," Holmes replied curtly. "The physician has declared it natural, the Yard perfunctory. And I am left to examine the remains of an altered scene."

We passed over Westminster Bridge, the Abbey dark against the greying sky, and soon pulled up at the arched gate of Lambeth. The ancient seat of England's prelates brooded over us, red-bricked and fortified, more castle than cathedral. A silent verger admitted us without word or question, his eyes noting the seal on our letter — but, with Anglican discretion, saying nothing of its Roman origin.

The Archbishop's study was a tall, narrow chamber, lined with theological texts and the faded maps of colonial dioceses. A slight odour of extinguished candles lingered in the air. The hearth had gone cold. The physician's work was done, the body removed, the room — in Holmes's view — already contaminated.

"I should have been called at once," he muttered, striding to the desk. "Now the body is gone, the servants scattered, the scene disturbed. What might have been learned is already lost to official haste."

He gestured to the floor. "There. Scuff marks suggest movement — not collapse. Someone was helped to the chair after the fact, or made to appear seated."

He stepped behind the desk. "And this—observe, Watson. The outline of a crucifix. Iron, most likely. Ripped from its mounting with haste."

I knelt to examine the wall. "The plaster is fractured. These rivet holes are torn inward. You think it was used?"

"Good day to you too, Lestrade," Holmes replied mildly. "The Yard has completed its investigations, have they not?"

Lestrade scowled. "Yes. But they did little more than tick the boxes and write it up as a stroke. I wasn't satisfied, so I returned on my own time." Lestrade

Holmes carried the small satchel containing the carved figurine

"I think," Holmes said, "that it was taken with purpose — and not by thieves."

We were still examining the wall when the door opened and Inspector Lestrade entered with his usual mix of civility and barely disguised irritation.

"Holmes," he said flatly. "I might have known."

continued, brushing water from his coat. "The attending physician found no signs of trauma. He put it down to the heart. We chalked it up accordingly."

"Then you closed the case?" Holmes asked.

Lestrade's expression tightened. "I didn't. That was the Superintendent's doing. But I wasn't satisfied. There's something... off about this one."

Holmes arched a brow. "And what now prompts your second thoughts?"

Lestrade hesitated, then drew a small notebook from his coat. "Had a word with one of the palace staff. Said His Grace had been receiving a visitor — a friar from Peckham, name of Madog. Welsh extraction. Bit of a mystery, that one. Comes and goes at odd hours. Not listed in the official schedule. Apparently, the Archbishop insisted he be shown in without announcement."

Holmes gave no sign of surprise. "And for this, you suspect him?"

Lestrade shrugged. "Well, look at it. Monk. Funny-sounding. Keeps odd hours. No known connections. Might be a zealot. I've seen quieter men do worse."

"Indeed," Holmes said dryly. "But have you seen men who distribute bread in the alleys of Peckham and visit the sick in all weather commit ecclesiastical murder with iron crucifixes?"

Lestrade's eyes narrowed. "So you've heard of him?"

"Only that which was offered discreetly," Holmes replied.

"And I find your reasoning — while imaginative — premature."

"Well," Lestrade said stiffly, "we'll see. If you find something better, I'll gladly hear it."

Holmes said nothing, but he turned back to the riveted wall with a sigh.

"Everything here has been touched. We have no record of the body's position, no measurement of lividity or time of death. What remains is inference, and inference grows weak when divorced from the moment."

"Then where shall we begin?"

Holmes replied, "We shall begin Watson in Peckham."

He turned back to Lestrade. "Should you arrest the friar, I suggest you do so quietly. If he is innocent, he will suffer enough from the suspicion."

"And if he's guilty?" Lestrade asked.

"Then," said Holmes, "he will suffer even more from meeting me."

Chapter III
The Franciscans of Peckham

he house of the Greyfriars of Our Lady of Dolours, tucked into a terrace near the bustle of Peckham High Street, presented more the character of a charitable mission than a monastic house. There was no cloistered hush, no stained glass, no tolling bell — only the clatter of a soup kitchen behind the gate and a boy delivering a basket of bread to a widow at the corner. The friars here belonged to an order descended from the Observant Franciscan tradition, only recently returned to England, and survived on donations, used books, and stubborn faith.

It was here that Friar Madog lived, preached, and — so Lestrade suspected — plotted the death of an archbishop.

The reception room where we were shown in bore no crucifix of gold or silver, only a worn wooden image of the Virgin and Child, and shelves of Latin theology beside a chipped kettle. The man who greeted us — Friar Madog — was slender, greying, and spoke in a tone barely louder than prayer. His habit, unmistakably grey, marked him as one of the wandering mendicants long vanished from English streets — until now.

"You come about His Grace of Lambeth," he said gently, motioning us to sit. "I had heard."

Holmes inclined his head. "You had been meeting with him regularly?"

"You are seeking answers," he said after Holmes had made our purpose known. "But I fear I can provide little. We spoke privately. He read deeply. Cranmer, More, Hilary of Poitiers. He asked about martyrdom. About Forest."

"John Forest?" I asked.

He nodded again, looking toward the hearth. "He was of my order. Burned at Smithfield. The tale is not much told in these parts — understandably. But the Archbishop found it... sobering. He said it was easy to forget the price men once paid for a bishop's collar."

Holmes leaned forward. "And did you encourage him in these thoughts?"

"This cross," he said, "is similar to the one that hung behind the Archbishop's chair. You recall it?"

Friar Madog was slender, greying, and spoke in a tone barely louder than prayer.

Madog met his gaze without defensiveness. "I answered his questions. I offered Mass for his intentions, with permission. I prayed with him. His Grace and I spoke in confidence."

Holmes raised an eyebrow. "On matters of faith?"

Madog bowed his head slightly. "On matters of conscience. I am not at liberty to say more."

Holmes allowed the silence to draw out, as he often did, then stepped to the shelf where a crucifix stood.

Madog looked up, surprised. "Yes of course. He said it brought him peace. It was... meaningful to him. Why do you ask?"

Holmes's voice was steady. "It is gone. Removed forcibly. The wall bears rivet-marks and splintered plaster."

Madog's face clouded. "That is troubling. I hope it has not been profaned."

"We hope the same," Holmes replied. "Your own visits to Lambeth — were they recent?"

"I visited three days ago, after dark. He sent word privately. We spoke for some time."

"May I ask what was discussed?"

Madog hesitated, then gently said, "Mr. Holmes, I do not believe it would be proper. The Archbishop did not speak to me as a politician or prelate, but as a man seeking clarity. I would betray that trust if I disclosed the substance of our conversation."

Holmes gave a single nod, not of agreement but of respect. "Very well. Then let me ask this: had he spoken of the beatification of Friar John Forest?"

Now the friar's expression changed.

"Yes. It had troubled him. Not the event itself — but the reaction it caused. Some among the English Church saw it as an insult. Others were drawn to it. The Archbishop seemed caught between duty and something deeper."

"Faith?" I asked.

Madog looked at me, and for the first time I sensed a trace of sadness behind the calm.

"No," he said quietly. "Fear."

"I did not murder him, if that is what you suspect."

"We suspect many things," Holmes replied.

"And what do you believe?"

Holmes stood and examined a shelf near the door. "I believe you are not the man Lestrade thinks you are. You are too still. Not in the way of artifice — but in the way of those who have made peace with themselves."

A moment passed. The friar seemed to accept this as a peculiar compliment.

"You preach in the streets," I said. "To the poor?"

"As I must," he replied. "The friary supports itself through donations and second hand books. We have no choir, no organ. Just soup and prayer."

Holmes moved to the door, pausing. "One last question. You carried, until recently, a small carved figure — a warrior saint. Saint Derfel or Derfel Gadarn as the Welsh would prefer."

Madog blinked in surprise. "Yes. Derfel. A soldier turned monk. I've carried him for years — carved by my uncle, who fought at Balaclava. It's a family relic as much as a spiritual one."

Holmes's eyes darkened. "You are quite sure you brought it back from your last visit to Lambeth?"

"I — yes. I remember touching it on the way home. It keeps me from dozing on the tram."

Holmes gave Watson a glance that spoke volumes.

The friar reached to his pocket, then stilled. "That's... strange. I always carry it."

"You are certain?"

"Yes." Madog stepped back, visibly shaken. "Do you believe someone took it?"

"I believe someone wants you to be seen differently than you are."

As we left the friary, the lamplighters had begun their evening rounds and the air turned sharp with chimney soot and night chill. Holmes was quiet until we reached the street, then said:

"He is not our man."

"You're certain?"

"Utterly. He is no zealot. He has nothing to gain and everything to lose. And most importantly — someone has taken pains to make him appear otherwise."

"You believe his conscience is clear?"

"No Watson," Holmes said softly. "But I believe it is burdened with the wrong crime."

Chapter IV
Torching a Forest

**ack** at Baker Street, Holmes plunged into a thick fog of reading, barely speaking as he pored over tomes from the dusty upper shelf labeled *Ecclesiastica*. Church histories, martyr lists, Tudor polemics — all were soon strewn across the carpet like so many shattered rosaries. He spoke little, smoked often, and occasionally hummed a psalm tune I did not recognise. I found myself poring over the same accounts, though with far less success in grasping the connections my friend so clearly saw coalescing before him.

It was just after supper when he looked up from a cracked quarto and said, "Did you know that Friar John Forest was beatified by the Pope not many years ago?"

"No," I replied. "Should I?"

Holmes tapped the spine of the book. "Not unless you are among the small coterie who follow the Vatican's decrees with devout precision. But to those within such circles — and

more crucially, to those without but watching warily — it was no small matter."

He pulled another book from the table and read aloud, his voice low and measured:

"On the twenty-second day of May, 1548, John Forest, Friar Minor of the Observant Order, was burned alive at Smithfield for denying the spiritual supremacy of the English Crown. His pyre was built upon the carved wooden figure of St. Derfel of Llandderfel — once a relic of Welsh piety, seized in Cromwell's purge and repurposed as kindling for the heretic's flesh."

He closed the book gently, as though it might sigh.

I shifted in my chair.

"They used a saint's statue as firewood?" I asked incredulously.

"Indeed Watson," Holmes replied. "A deliberate act of desecration. The old faith reduced to ash, and the man with it."

I looked down at the rug, disturbed. "But this was done in the name of reform. By our own Church."

Holmes arched a brow. "Your Church, Watson. The Church of England, in its infancy — bold, bloody, and terribly afraid of its parent."

The fire cracked.

He reached for the Derfel figurine, still resting in the tray where he had placed it. "And now, four centuries later, the Roman Church declares that same friar — Forest — to be *blessed*. A martyr. A confessor of truth. The statue used to burn him has vanished into legend, and the man himself now walks the liturgical calendar."

The old faith reduced to ash, and the man with it.

I shifted uncomfortably. "I had always imagined... progress. A casting off of error. But this— this is barbarity."

Holmes studied me for a moment. "Faiths are not judged by their founding myths, Watson, but by the violence they forget."

He turned the figure in his hands.

"It is no surprise that such a gesture has rattled certain English nerves."

"You think the beatification caused offence?"

"I think it reignited an old fire. There are those who see the Archbishop's private interest in Forest's story not as curiosity, but as sympathy. And sympathy, in such a man, can look very like treason."

"And the figure of Derfel?"

"Planted," said Holmes. "Deliberately. It ties Friar Madog to Forest — to martyrdom, to sedition. It makes him seem a firebrand, when all he is, is a servant."

He pored over tomes from the dusty upper shelf labelled Ecclesiastica.

Holmes stood and walked slowly to the mantel, placing the figurine beside his tobacco jar.

"Someone fears Rome's shadow lengthening once more across English soil. And they believe Montague was preparing to step into it."

I said nothing for some time. The image of a man burned atop his own saints haunted me.

"Then who planted it?"

Holmes turned to face me. "Someone who knows this history as well as I do. And someone far closer to the Archbishop's hearth than the friar of Peckham ever was."

Chapter V
Staff and Secrets

**he** following morning found us once again in a hansom, this time bound not for Peckham, but for Lambeth Palace — that venerable seat of Anglican power, a bastion of an older England. Holmes was uncharacteristically silent as we approached the gates, his mind clearly sifting through fragments, faces, and half-formed patterns.

We were received without fanfare, though with an odd mixture of deference and wariness. Scotland Yard had already come and gone, leaving behind a residue of suspicion and paperwork but little in the way of conclusions. The death, for now, was being treated as a "sudden and tragic heart failure," though few among the staff truly believed it.

A senior canon with a limp and a distracted manner provided us a ledger of household names, as well as access to the late

Archbishop's study, now locked and shrouded in a funereal hush. But it was not the rooms or their contents that drew Holmes's

focus now. It was the men and women who moved through them.

Over the next two hours, Holmes spoke with a series of household staff — the verger, the butler, a pair of footmen, a cleaning girl, and the housekeeper — in tones varying from brusque to disarmingly affable. He asked little about the crime and much about habits: the Archbishop's reading hours, his walking paths, his visitors, his silences. Names were mentioned, routines charted. But it was a particular name — uttered with quiet respect and equal caution — that recurred with unmistakable significance:

"Mr. Hargrave."

He was the Archbishop's personal secretary, and had been for seven years. A reserved, meticulous man of about forty, he was said to possess a "churchman's spine" and a "librarian's manner." He rarely left the grounds, ate simply, and was often found in the small garden behind the south transept, reading devotional works or taking dictation beneath the plane trees.

Holmes asked to see him immediately.

We found Mr. Hargrave seated in the late Archbishop's anteroom, sorting correspondence into trays. He rose at once, tall, neatly dressed in a dark suit with a high collar, and with eyes that gave the impression of intense internal weather behind a perfectly calm surface.

"Gentlemen," he said, "I understand you are assisting with... the inquiry."

Holmes gave a small bow. "Only unofficially. We seek clarity — and hope to avoid scandal."

"A noble hope," Hargrave replied, before gesturing us into the adjoining room.

What followed was a conversation marked by guarded civility. Hargrave answered all questions, but not without careful curation.

"Yes, His Grace had been troubled of late. No, he did not speak much of it. Yes, there were visitors from Rome. Yes, he had grown contemplative. No, I do not believe he intended anything dramatic."

Hargrave answered all questions, but not without careful curation.

Holmes let the interview meander gently toward books. Hargrave perked slightly.

"His Grace had been reading Newman again," the secretary noted. "*Apologia*, mostly. And some of the Tractarian sermons."

"He admired Newman?"

Hargrave's mouth drew tight. "He admired his courage. Though some here feared he admired... other things."

"Such as?" Holmes asked lightly.

Hargrave hesitated.

"There were whispers, Mr. Holmes. Suggestions. The sort that begin in chapel pews and end in corridors. Some joked that we had 'a new Newman' in the Palace."

Holmes said nothing, but I saw the flicker in his eye.

When we departed, Holmes requested — with the Canon's reluctant permission — access to Hargrave's work room. It was modest: tidy shelves, filing cabinets, prayer cards, and a locked drawer (quickly opened by Holmes with no one the wiser). Inside: three blank folios, one ink-stained glove, and a small journal.

Holmes leafed through the journal with surgical precision. Most of it was mundane — Latin phrases, sermon summaries, correspondence drafts. But here and there were odd jottings in the margins:

"Rome is creeping in — silently."

"Confession is not dialogue. It is surrender."

"He will undo everything. Even Cranmer. Even Ridley."

Holmes closed the book and held it in silence.

"Well?" I asked.

"He is a scholar," Holmes said softly. "But also, I think, a zealot. One driven not by ambition, but fear."

"Fear of what?"

"Of betrayal Watson. Of watching a ship he served steer into foreign waters. His loyalty to the Church is unquestioned — but his vision of it is fragile. To him, Montague was not a bishop who doubted. He was a traitor who paused before crossing the Alps."

I glanced around the quiet, stone-walled chamber. The gloom felt heavier.

"And if he feared that betrayal might become real?"

Holmes nodded.

"Then he may have chosen to act — in the name of the Church he thought was being forsaken."

Lambeth Palace, seat of the Archbishop of Canterbury

Chapter VI
A Letter from the Fire

t was a damp and disagreeable morning in Baker Street, one of those London dawns when the fog seems to seep through the very brickwork, and even the fire crackles with reluctance. I had just rung for breakfast and was poring over the headlines in *The Times* when Mrs. Hudson appeared, balancing a silver tray and a disapproving expression.

"I do wish, Mr. Holmes," she said, setting down the kippers and toast with more force than necessary, "that you'd eat something more regular. Not three black coffees and a pipe for supper. It's unnatural."

Holmes, hunched by the window with his pipe already between his lips, gave a vague grunt.

"And that dreadful Persian slipper under the mantle again," she added, her voice sharpening. "Reeking of tobacco and dust. I'll not have it fouling my hearth."

"I require consistency in my ashes," Holmes replied without turning.

"You'll require a physician if you keep this up," she muttered, then nodded to me with exaggerated civility. "Doctor."

"I do my best," I said, though the battle for Holmes's habits was one I had long since ceased to fight.

Mrs. Hudson left in a flurry of starch and indignation. Holmes continued to smoke in silence, eyes unfocused, until a small rustle at the door caught our attention.

A single folded note had been slipped beneath the threshold.

Holmes rose, retrieved it, and opened the paper without comment. After a moment, he handed it to me, his brow furrowed.

"The friar's zeal has overcome his discretion. He would avenge the fire with fire. Look to his words, and you will see the truth. Confession is not peace."

The language was ecclesiastical, almost sermon-like. My eyes met Holmes's. "It must be about Friar Madog."

"That," Holmes replied, "is the writer's intention."

We had barely time to speculate further before Mrs. Hudson appeared at the door, announcing that Inspector Lestrade was climbing the stairs two at a time.

"Morning, gentlemen," Lestrade puffed, removing his hat and shaking off the drizzle. "I daresay we've cracked it."

"Indeed?" Holmes said, without rising from his chair.

Lestrade produced a folded sheet of paper from his coat pocket. "Found this tucked inside the late Archbishop's psalter in the chapel. And signed, no less." He smoothed it out on the desk with all the triumph of a magician revealing his final card.

Holmes and I leaned in. The letter read:

"I have longed for justice, even vengeance. For Forest. For the martyrs who burned while England knelt to kings. If the fire must be lit again to cleanse this land, then let it begin here, with a bishop who would betray Rome once more."

Signed in blockish script: *Fr. Madog.*

Lestrade looked up, beaming. "There's your motive. There's your confession. The man's got a chip on his shoulder about the

Lestrade produced a folded sheet of paper from his coat pocket.

Reformation, he's been lurking round the Archbishop, and now he's put it all in writing. Bit florid, if you ask me, but the courts won't mind that."

Holmes was quiet. He took the sheet gently and examined it under the gaslight. Then, almost absently, he retrieved the earlier anonymous note from the desk and placed the two side by side.

"Both typewritten," I observed.

"Indeed," Holmes murmured. "And remarkably so. Note the slight nick in the lower loop of the 'g'—here, and here."

He reached into a drawer and produced a small envelope. "I obtained a sample from Mr. Hargrave's study," he said. "His typewriter — a German Imperial, uncommon here — has a damaged typebar. It leaves a distinctive mark."

Lestrade frowned. "You're saying he forged it?"

Holmes's voice remained mild. "I am saying only that the author of both these letters had access to that particular machine. And a keen sense of drama."

Lestrade waved him off. "All speculation. We've got what we need — confession, motive, proximity. Scotland Yard's quite satisfied."

Holmes gave a small, un-readable smile. "Then by all means, Inspector. Proceed as you see fit."

Lestrade tucked the letter into his coat with a satisfied snap and took his leave, muttering some-thing about warrants and chain of custody.

We waited until his footsteps faded.

Holmes turned to me at once. "Madog is innocent, of course."

"Of course," I replied. "You've known since—?"

"Since the phrasing," Holmes said, taking back the forged letter and reading aloud: "'Cleanse this land... betrayal... fire must be lit again.' It is the rhetoric of apocalypse, not reconciliation. A Franciscan — especially one of Madog's humility — would speak of sorrow, not vengeance. And he would never invoke flame as justice. That language belongs to another mind entirely."

He set both pages down, flattening them with care.

"Besides," he added, "the typeface tells us more than the tongue. The real author is not only a liar, but also a fool for thinking I would not look closely."

"And now?"

Holmes stood. "Now we bait the final hook. Hargrave has taken great pains to paint Madog as a fanatic. It's time we let him believe he's succeeded — and see what else he might do when he thinks he's won."

German Imperial typewriter

Chapter VII
The Garden Trap

**olmes** spent the following day in a state of quiet agitation — not the tempestuous sort which led him to violin scraping or chemical mischief, but the subtler, more dangerous stillness of a hunter testing the tension of his own snare. I had seen this mood before: in Dartmoor, before the hound broke cover; in Whitehall, before the downfall of a civil servant who fancied himself too clever by half.

By late afternoon, he had issued two telegrams, one note to the Papal Nuncio (written in Latin, sealed with wax), and a third to Scotland Yard requesting Lestrade's discreet cooperation. Then, turning to me with a glint behind his pale eyes, he said:

"Put on your warmest coat, Watson. We have an appointment with the shadows."

"Shall I take my revolver Holmes"

"I think not Watson", replied Holmes. "Our prey holds no danger for us I believe. Besides I have already altered Lestrade."

Lambeth Palace, by night, is a different creature from its daytime self. The crowds are gone, the corridors hollow and hushed, the air thick with the scent of stone and old paper. Beneath the pale flicker of gas lamps.

"The Nuncio," Holmes explained as we approached Lambeth under cover of darkness, "has not only a sharp theological mind, but a diplomatic reach as well. He conveyed our intentions to the Sub-Dean — a man with no love of scandal, nor appetite for police trampling over consecrated ground. We have, for now, quiet leave to make our inquiries. But no torches, no fanfare, and not a word to the press."

Holmes led us through a side entrance secured with Papal approval — or, more precisely, Papal discretion. We passed silently along the cloister and into the south garden, a modest walled green behind the chapel where the late Archbishop had often taken solitary walks. There, beneath a plane tree blackened by years and soot, stood an iron brazier, filled with a modest pile of ash and un-burnt paper. A small bench sat nearby, where Montague had once read evening prayers.

Holmes produced a single sheet of parchment from within his coat.

"What is it?" I asked.

"Something Hargrave cannot resist," he replied.

"How will he know to look there?" I asked.

Holmes smiled faintly. "I have slipped a note — appearing to be written by Montague himself — into Hargrave's daily correspondence. It mentions 'a draft left near the garden brazier — to be burned unread.' If Hargrave's nerves are as frayed as I suspect, he'll be drawn to it like a moth to a flame."

Holmes slid the page halfway into the brazier, letting just enough of it protrude that it might tempt a hurried glance. Written upon it — in Montague's own hand, as expertly forged by Holmes himself — were a few fragmentary phrases:

"...no longer can I pretend... the claims of Rome weigh heavier than the ghosts of Cranmer... ...to declare for unity of the faith at whatever cost... ...the Nuncio awaits my answer..."

Beside it, Holmes left a monogrammed corner torn from Montague's writing folio, already smeared with wax — just enough to lend authenticity.

We retreated into the shadows.

"You're sure he won't send someone else?" I asked.

Holmes shook his head. "Hargrave is not a conspirator, Watson — he's a zealot. He trusts no one but himself. If he believes that damning proof lies unburned beneath the Archbishop's garden tree, then he will come. And he will come alone."

The hours passed. The garden grew colder. I confess I dozed at one point, waking with a start to find Holmes unmoved, eyes fixed on the darkened door across the courtyard.

Then — just past midnight — we heard it. A soft creak of a door. The faint crunch of steps across gravel. A tall figure emerged: Mr. Hargrave, cloaked, gloved, head lowered. He moved with nervous deliberation, pausing once, then making directly for the brazier.

He bent, seized the sheet, and read.

I saw his hand tremble.

Then, with sudden fury, he struck a match — lit it against the brazier's edge, and tried to set the page alight.

"Now, Lestrade," Holmes spoke.

The inspector and two constables emerged from the dark like avenging shades. Hargrave spun, startled — and dropped the flaming paper into the ash. Holmes was upon it at once, retrieving the page with iron tongs and dousing the flame. The text remained legible.

Hargrave stared at him, mouth agape.

"You wanted to destroy it," Holmes said quietly. "Because it confirmed your fear — that the Archbishop was preparing to leave the Church of England. And that fear turned to loathing."

Hargrave said nothing.

Holmes stepped forward. "You wrote the letter framing Madog. You planted it in the psalter. You borrowed his rhetoric and twisted it into menace. And when even that failed to rouse a charge, you came to ensure that

"Now, Lestrade," Holmes uttered.

the Archbishop's secret would die with him."

Lestrade stepped forward, handcuffs in hand.

But Hargrave did not move. His face had gone pale, his voice thin and cold.

"He was going to betray England," he whispered. "He called Rome the mother church. Do you understand what that means?"

"I understand," Holmes said grimly. "That you believed your faith justified murder. That you killed a man who trusted you, in the name of a Church he never left."

Hargrave's voice trembled. "He was going to undo Cranmer. Undo everything."

Lestrade placed a hand on his shoulder. "Come along now, Mr. Hargrave."

As they led him away, he murmured something I could not hear. But Holmes, still watching, shook his head.

"Avenging Cranmer," he said. "As if the flames of Smithfield had not burned long enough."

Chapter VIII
The Secretary's Confession

**he** dawn was a pallid smear on the Thames by the time we returned to Baker Street. Hargrave had been taken into custody, silent and unmoving, his eyes fixed not on his captors but on the crumpled page Holmes had retrieved from the flames.

We said little on the cab ride home. Holmes sat with his chin sunk into his collar, the forged confession clutched in one gloved hand like a relic exhumed from a tomb. Only when we reached the hearth did he speak.

"It was always going to be Hargrave," he said. "But I had hoped, foolishly perhaps, that the death of a man of peace would not turn another to fire."

Two days passed before the formal interview. Scotland Yard, unsure how to navigate a case that touched both Lambeth and Rome, allowed Holmes to conduct the interrogation under their supervision. I was permitted to attend.

Hargrave sat in a small room at the Yard, composed but pale, his hands folded before him. There was no sign of remorse, nor of the defiance we had seen in the garden. He looked, I thought, like a man in mourning — for something other than the Archbishop.

Holmes was direct.

"You confronted Edmund Montague in his private chapel. You raised the iron crucifix — wrenched from his own wall — and demanded he renounce his thoughts of Rome."

Hargrave did not speak.

"You did not strike him," Holmes continued. "But you threatened him — and in that moment, his heart gave out. A natural death, as the physician concluded — but provoked by unnatural terror."

Still, Hargrave said nothing.

Holmes held up the cross. "This was found in the mud of the Thames just below Lambeth. No blow was dealt, but the circumstances speak — and you know it."

At first it seems he might remain silent. Then Hargrave's lips moved. "He was going to convert." It was barely a whisper.

"You believed that. But you had no proof."

"I had enough," he whispered. "He quoted Newman. He wrote of 'returning to the fold.' He met with the Nuncio in secret. He dismissed my concerns. What more was I to do?"

"You were to trust him," Holmes said, his voice low. "Or at the very least, not terrorise a frail man into his grave."

Hargrave's tone sharpened. "He would have betrayed the Church of England. He would have handed it back to Rome — to incense and idols and foreign tongues. The Church made him a shepherd, and he became a Judas."

"You took a symbol of faith," Holmes said, holding the iron cross aloft, "and made it into a weapon."

"I never struck him," Hargrave hissed. "I held it — yes — I tore it from the wall and begged him to swear he would not forsake the Church. I asked him to remember Cranmer. He clutched his chest and collapsed. I never touched him."

Lestrade, who had been silent in the corner, stepped forward. "You forged the letters. You tried to frame the friar."

Hargrave's expression hardened. "He had already infected the Archbishop's thinking. He spoke of martyrs — of England's guilt. If not now, then soon, Montague would have crossed to Rome. I saw the path laid before him."

"You feared what might happen," Holmes said, "and so you made yourself executioner for a crime that had not yet occurred."

"I did what I had to," Hargrave muttered. "No one else would act. Not the bishops, not the laity. Someone had to guard the gates."

Lestrade shook his head. "You'll have time to reflect behind them."

As the Inspector left to summon the constables, Hargrave turned to Holmes. "He would have undone everything. You don't understand."

Holmes stared at him, his voice cold. "No. You don't

understand. Faith without humility is no faith at all. It is merely power, dressed in liturgy."

* * * * * * * * * * *

Later that week, Friar Madog was quietly released. There was no apology, but a note from the Papal Nuncio assured Holmes that the Vatican was "most grateful." Madog had already returned to Peckham, where we found him weeding the mission garden beside a weathered statue of Saint Francis.

Holmes approached without

"He died of the heart," Holmes said simply. "But the cause was no act of God."

Madog bowed his head. "May the Church learn to listen to hearts as well as books."

Holmes offered a silent nod.

Watson and I turned to go. Behind us, the friar knelt once more to tend to the roses — grey-robed, weathered, and still.

"May the Church learn to listen to hearts as well as books."

ceremony.

Chapter IX
A Bitter Peace

**here** was no trial.

Such matters, when they brush too close to ecclesiastical walls, are not always resolved in courtrooms. Mr. Hargrave was declared medically unfit to stand before a jury — his mind, the attending alienist said, "disordered by zeal and burdened by religious mania." He was quietly committed to a sanatorium in the south, where he remains to this day under Church supervision.

No further public statements were made by Lambeth Palace. No pastoral letter. No mention of Hargrave's confession or of the late Archbishop's possible leanings toward Rome. The Church of England, having nearly glimpsed its own fracture in the mirror, chose instead to avert its gaze.

The Papal Nuncio expressed "relief that peace had been restored," and made no public comment. There was no mention of the cooperation that had occurred. Whatever Rome had feared in Montague's death, it too chose silence over confrontation.

I confess that the resolution, if one may call it that, left me unsettled.

Holmes, however, was unbothered. He had never sought applause, and in this case, seemed particularly content to let the affair recede from view.

"Some truths," he remarked to me one morning, as he rearranged his clippings in the scrapbook, "are like old cathedrals. Admired from the outside — best left unexamined within."

Friar Madog continues his work at Our Lady of Dolours in Peckham. I am told his sermons have grown gentler, more pastoral, less burdened by the iron heat of martyrdom. He did not speak again of John Forest, though he kept a small icon of the saint in his cell.

The Derfel Gadarn figurine, worn and blackened, now rests on Holmes's mantelpiece, half-buried among a clutter of cases past — a fossil from a chapter of history most would rather forget.

I asked him once why he had kept it.

"It reminds me," he said, "that even saints have swords — and that the past is never entirely buried, only shelved."

There the matter rests.

If Montague's death was a murder, it was one committed in the shadows of theology, where justice and truth are but pilgrims passing through. The Anglican Church buried its Archbishop with honour. Rome offered no challenge. And in the space between the two, Holmes lit his pipe and filed another case away.

It was a bitter peace. But peace, nonetheless.

Some truths are best left unexamined.

The Sign of the Sacrament

Chapter I
Smoke Among the Spires

**t** was on a raw and sooty afternoon in late October that I found my friend Mr. Sherlock Holmes in an unusually reflective state. The fire had burned low, and the only light in the sitting room at Baker Street came from the grey gleam beyond the curtains and the faint glow of the gas lamp Holmes had neglected to turn up. He sat in his armchair, legs crossed, his long fingers steepled beneath his chin, the smoke from his pipe curling toward the ceiling like incense from some troubled altar.

"I suppose," I ventured, "that London has given you nothing today but fog, ash, and boredom?"

"There is always pattern, Watson," Holmes murmured. "Even in soot."

At that precise moment, Mrs. Hudson appeared bearing an envelope — thick, cream-coloured, sealed with red wax and stamped with the unmistakable ring of the Vatican. Holmes raised an eyebrow. I saw at once the handwriting was not English.

"A curious emissary," he said, examining the seal. "I've only received one such before — the case of murder in the Vatican, as you recall."

I did recall — though it was one of those adventures I had been asked to seal from public view. I was more surprised that Holmes had not already unsealed the letter.

"Well?" I prompted.

Smiling at my impatience, Holmes broke the wax with a delicate flourish and read. His eyes narrowed. Then he stood abruptly, tossing the letter into my lap.

Gentile Signor Holmes,

Your name has been invoked in grave and urgent matters. Three men of the cloth — servants of the Church and of the poor — have been murdered in Whitechapel. The manner of their deaths is too violent, too symbolically charged, to be dismissed as mere slum violence. We fear a deeper cause, and a deeper peril.

We implore your assistance. His Holiness sends his confidence and prayers.

— Monsignor Paolo, Private Secretary to His Holiness, Leo PP XIII

I looked up. "Three murdered? In Whitechapel? But the news makes no mention—"

"Because the city sees what it wishes to see," Holmes replied. "The press would rather publish lies about anarchists and Fenian plots than admit to ritualistic killings of priests in the shadow of St Mary and St Michael."

He walked to the mantel, absently stirring the ashes in the grate. "I have been following these deaths for weeks, Watson. I half-expected this missive from Rome — in fact, I rather wondered what had taken them so long to write. Each killing has been marked by a peculiar symbolism, and each victim served in one of the poorest Catholic parishes in the East End. There is an order in the choice of victims, and I fear there will be more."

"Then why have you not acted?" I demanded.

His expression hardened. "Because I was otherwise engaged on a matter touching

An envelope — thick, cream-coloured, sealed with red wax and stamped with the unmistakable ring of the Vatican.

the Crown — one of those unfortunate situations where the fate of an empire outweighs the fate of a few. I regret the delay, Watson, more than I can express. The Vatican's request merely confirms what I already knew: that the hour for observation is over."

His brow furrowed. "It is not merely crime they fear, Watson. It is the possibility of sacrilege — calculated, theatrical sacrilege."

I confess, I felt a chill not attributable to the autumn air.

"And so they've come to you?"

Holmes nodded. "When Rome sends no guards, it sends silence. That silence has now reached Baker Street. I must go to the East End. You, of course, will accompany me."

He knocked the spent ash from his pipe. "Bring your revolver, Watson — and your stoutest boots. The streets around St Mary and St Michael are not for the faint of heart."

Chapter II
Among the Flock

**rey** skies hung over the East End like damp wool, muting even the occasional clang of a tram bell. Holmes and I passed from the cobbled arteries of Aldgate into narrower streets where the air grew thick with coal smoke, fish oil, and the restless murmur of the Irish poor. Barefoot children darted between market stalls, dodging the wheels of costermongers' carts. Here and there, rosary beads dangled from rough hands, and the scarlet sashes of temperance societies swayed over patched coats.

Holmes's sharp gaze shifted abruptly to my right-hand pocket. "Best return that, my lad," he said without looking at the boy who had appeared beside me like a shadow. The child froze mid-fumble, eyes wide as Holmes's long fingers closed lightly — but firmly — around his wrist. With a twist, the pickpocket's loot (my pocket watch) was returned, and the boy vanished into the crowd like smoke on a breeze.

"They start young here," I muttered.

"They start young because they must," Holmes replied curtly.

We pressed on, and I could not help but think of the Irish tide that had rolled into London these past decades — refugees of famine, now builders of roads, diggers of sewers, dock labourers, costermongers, and navvies. They carried the city's weight on their shoulders yet were regarded by many Londoners as lazy, drunken, or worse.

As if reading my thoughts, Holmes's head turned sharply. "Watson, it is the curse of the unimaginative to mistake necessity for vice. These men do not drink because they are Irish — they drink because a man who works sixteen hours in filth will take whatever warmth is offered to him. Replace the gin-shop with a clean bed and a fair wage, and you will see how quickly the 'Irish vice' evaporates."

He gave a thin smile. "There are voices in Rome, I hear, speaking of just such reforms — of the rights of labour, of the duties of the wealthy toward the poor. If ever such counsel reaches the ears of our industrial barons, it will be a new thing indeed."

weathered cassock, his black hair flecked with grey, his eyes hard as flint. "And I tell you, Mr. Rourke," he said, "your quarrel is with injustice, not with the Church that clothes your

"They start young because they must," Holmes replied curtly.

Our destination loomed ahead: St Mary and St Michael's, its steeple shouldering through the smog. Outside the gates, a knot of men had gathered, their voices raised in argument. Snatches of speech reached us — "landlords' lackeys," "the Pope's chain," "freedom for the working man" — until one voice cut through the rest.

The speaker was a tall, broad-shouldered priest in a

children and buries your dead."

The man he addressed — Declan Rourke — had the clenched fists and flushed cheeks of a born street-fighter. "You bind the workers to their misery with your prayers and your holy water," he spat. "Better a free man's hunger than a slave's supper."

It was then the priest's gaze flicked to us, and the hardness softened. "Mr. Holmes, I presume? I had word from a friend of the Church that you might be sent. Though I confess, I expected Rome to delay longer."

Holmes inclined his head slightly. "Father Keogh, I believe. Rome may be slow, but her letters cross my path in unexpected ways."

Keogh stepped forward, offering a firm hand. "You'll have heard of these killings. Don't let anyone tell you they're the work of chance. These are the knives of anarchists, men who'd see the whole Church burn so they can dance in its ashes. And I'll name you the worst of them — Rourke here."

Rourke's glare shifted to Holmes, who regarded him with infuriating calm. "Your hands, Mr. Rourke?" Holmes asked abruptly.

The Irishman held them out, puzzled. Holmes inspected them, then nodded. "A fighter's calluses, yes. But not the precision of a killer who leaves a mock benediction. No — I should think you break jaws, not hearts."

Keogh looked at Holmes sharply. "Then you don't believe it's political?"

"I believe," Holmes said, "that politics is a convenient cloak — one that can cover more than one shape beneath it."

Chapter III
Enter Bookworm Brown

**he** parish library was a long, narrow chamber above the sacristy, its air heavy with the mingled scents of candle wax, leather bindings, and coal smoke seeping through the ill-fitting window frames. Dust motes danced in the weak shafts of light filtering through grimy panes, lending the room a reluctant sanctity.

Father Keogh ushered us inside. "If you want the truth about our dead men, Mr Holmes, you'll find more here than in any police report."

From behind a stack of ledgers emerged a slight figure in a threadbare black coat, arms piled high with books. He looked scarcely twenty, with a pale, intelligent face half-hidden by round spectacles.

"This is Brown," Keogh said. "A final year seminarian, and a fine scholar — and the only one who can find anything in this chaos. Others call him 'Bookworm'."

Brown inclined his head shyly. "A title I've earned, Father."

Holmes's gaze fell upon the volumes in his arms: Aquinas, Newman, and — to my surprise — a treatise on criminal anthropology. "An interesting course of study," Holmes observed.

"One must understand the mind of evil to combat it," Brown replied, adjusting the books. "If I am to serve the Church well, I must know the wolf as well as the shepherd knows the flock."

Holmes's eyes brightened with approval. "Quite so."

Setting the books down, Brown unrolled a set of sketches. "I copied these before the constable's files... vanished." His tone made it clear this was no accident.

He pointed to the first sketch. "Father Malloy: throat cut, hands arranged in blessing — but note the streak of wax on the index finger. Too deliberate to be accidental."

The second drawing showed Friar Donnelly, found in the vestry. "Heart removed," Brown said quietly. "Positioned facing the altar. No signs of robbery, though his crucifix was gone."

The third, Brother Finnegan, discovered in the alley behind the church. "Same throat wound, but the head was turned sharply left. And here—" Brown indicated a faint smudge near the left palm — "traces of ash. Not from the street; too fine. Likely incense."

assumed the candles were lit after death. I suggest the inverse — they were lit before, and the victim forced to hold them. That would explain the splatter pattern here."

Brown blinked, processing, then nodded slowly.

It was rare for Holmes to offer correction without disdain, but I could not help noticing how readily he warmed to the young man's insight. For reasons I could not quite name, I felt a pang — perhaps the same mild jealousy a student feels when

"An interesting course of study," Holmes observed.

Holmes bent over the papers, tapping one long finger on the wax mark. "Your observation is acute, Mr Brown. Yet you've

seeing his teacher turn to a newer pupil.

Holmes rolled up the sketches with care. "Mr Brown, you have given me something the official inquiry has not: evidence worth the name. I think we may do fine work together."

satisfaction of having been understood.

Church of St Mary and St Michael, Whitechapel, London

Brown flushed at the praise, though his eyes betrayed no vanity — only the quiet

Chapter IV
The Crimson Circle

**he** call came by telephone — a recent intrusion into Baker Street life that Mrs Hudson detested as a vulgar, jangling nuisance. She had been all for having the instrument removed until the night her sister in Kensington used it to summon assistance when a lodger collapsed. Since then, she merely sniffed at it whenever it rang.

It was just after breakfast when the bell sounded. Holmes lifted the receiver with a curt, "Yes?" A moment later he replaced it and was already reaching for his coat. "Another murder, Watson. At St Mary and St Michael itself — during the small hours, and within the church walls. Scotland Yard can no longer dismiss these as dockside stabbings."

We hailed a hansom in Baker Street, the horse's breath steaming in the raw morning air. As we rattled eastward through streets still slick from overnight rain, Holmes sat back with his chin buried in the folds of his scarf, eyes half closed.

"You are thinking of a suspect already?" I ventured.

"I am thinking," Holmes replied, "of the mind required to commit such acts — and of the mind required to disguise them as something else. You see, Watson, there is a danger in assuming these murders are born of passion or drunken violence. Passion is messy, random. This is deliberate, composed — a hand that writes the same word over and over in blood, and in the same script."

"You believe it is one man, then?"

"Indubitably. And one with a purpose beyond murder. Consider: a priest slain in the street may be explained by chance misfortune. A priest slain within the very precincts of his church? That is a declaration — one intended to strike at the heart of the faithful." He gave a short, humourless laugh. "The press may bluster about anarchists, but whoever holds this knife is a far colder breed."

The cab jolted to a halt in a street lined with hawkers and ragged children, the spire of St Mary and St Michael rising like a pale finger in the mist.

By the time we reached the great doors, bolted against the crowd outside, a knot of women in shawls were murmuring prayers, the smell of paraffin and wet cobblestones heavy in the air. Inside, Lestrade was waiting. "Couldn't keep this one quiet," he told Holmes grimly. "A priest butchered in his own confessional."

Friar Patrick Byrne's body sat slumped against the lattice, his cassock soaked, his head bowed as though awaiting absolution. Before him on the stone floor was a perfect circle, drawn in his blood, with a cross cut cleanly through its centre.

Holmes knelt beside the grisly emblem, his gaze roving. "Meticulous... far too meticulous for the rabble you've been questioning, Lestrade."

"I've heard that before," Lestrade muttered. "You going to tell me about the wax again?"

Holmes's tone sharpened. "The missing wax was from the first killing, and its absence was no accident. The constable on the scene recorded it — a fragment of white altar candle in the victim's palm — and yet by the time the evidence reached the Yard, it had vanished from the docket. I am told the same happened in the second case. And now—" He gestured to the circle. "—the pattern continues, bolder."

A quiet voice came from behind us. "This is not merely a pattern, Mr Holmes." It was Brown, the young seminarian, his eyes fixed on the blood-marked floor. "The circle stands for eternity; the cross, for salvation. Here they are inverted, in blood, before the altar. A deliberate parody of the Holy Sacrament."

Holmes glanced at him approvingly. "An astute reading, Mr Brown. You are correct — though you have yet to note the stroke order. The cross was drawn right to left. Our killer is left-handed."

Lestrade gave a doubtful grunt. "Left-handed or not, it still smells of Fenian trouble-making to me."

Holmes rose, dusting his knees. "No, Inspector. These killings are not born of the heat of politics. They are cool, calculated sermons written in blood."

"A priest butchered in his own confessional."

Chapter V
The Fires of Rourke

**wo** days had passed since our meeting in the parish library, and the grey pall of East London seemed heavier still. A telegram from Brown had reached Baker Street that morning — the young seminarian claimed to have stumbled upon a fresh clue, one he believed Holmes would "find consistent with the pattern."

Mrs Hudson, who still had not forgiven the intrusion of the telephone into her orderly domain, relayed the message with a sniff. Holmes hailed a hansom, and we set off toward the East End, the autumn drizzle streaking the cab windows.

Lestrade intercepted us on Commercial Street, emerging from the murk with the purposeful tread of a man who thought he had already solved the case.

"Holmes!" he called, striding toward us. "Our Irish firebrand is up to his old tricks. Declan Rourke — caught him last night daubing 'No Pope' across the doors of a soup kitchen. Paint on his hands, knife in his belt, and half the neighbourhood roused by his shouting."

Holmes raised an eyebrow. "Vandalism and bluster, Lestrade. I grant you his voice carries, but his hands? They lack the cold discipline to carry out the murders we have seen."

Lestrade ignored the rebuke and continued. "You've met him — always riling up the dockers, giving speeches about throwing off Rome's chains. He's been organising protest meetings, too. Claims the priests keep the Irish poor docile so the landlords can bleed them dry."

Holmes's eyes narrowed. "And yet when the killings occurred, the victims' hands bore traces of candle wax — ritual candles, used after death. That's not Rourke's style. He's a man of impulse, not ceremony."

We resumed our way toward the church, Lestrade trailing reluctantly. The hansom jolted over the cobbles, the driver cursing under his breath at a fish cart blocking the lane. Through the narrow streets we passed lines of tenements where laundry hung limp in the damp air and barefoot children played in the gutters.

Holmes gazed out the window, speaking almost to himself. "The English think of the Irish here as beasts of burden — cheap labour for the docks, the railways, the factories. And yet it is in their chapels and kitchens that the heart of this community beats. To strike at their priests is to strike at their very identity."

When we reached St Mary and St Michael, Brown was waiting in the doorway, his arms full of books and pamphlets. "Mr Holmes," he said eagerly, "I think you will wish to see these

— and not only for the sake of Rourke's innocence."

Among the bundle were Rourke's tracts — ill-printed, furious in tone, littered with crude slogans — and a thin, older pamphlet written in a far cooler, sharper hand. Holmes scanned its pages, his expression shifting from curiosity to certainty.

"Watson," he said quietly, "this is no dockside screed. This is the voice of our murderer."

This is the voice of our murderer.

Chapter VI
The Protestant Mask

olmes turned the thin pamphlet over in his hands as we moved into the vestry, Brown placing the rest of the bundle on a scarred oak table. The tracts from Rourke were smeared with ink and outrage; this one was different. Its paper was heavier, its type clean and deliberate, its rhetoric stripped of all passion and yet carrying a venom far more dangerous.

"Note the Latin tags," Holmes said, tapping the margin with a long finger. "No dockside rabble-rouser wrote this. Here we have the hand of a trained theologian, educated in the higher mysteries, and now perverting them."

Brown adjusted his spectacles. "The passages against 'the papistical blasphemy of the Mass'—this is not the common Protestant polemic. Whoever wrote this has taken aim at the sacraments themselves, not merely the Church's authority."

"Indeed," Holmes replied. "And you will observe the peculiar symbol impressed faintly in the paper grain — a circle with a cross through it. The same that was drawn in blood upon the floor of the confessional."

Lestrade, who had followed us in, gave a sceptical snort. "Aye, it's fancy talk, but it's still an Irish knife that did the work, mark me."

Holmes ignored him. "This symbol was not invented by Rourke or any Fenian firebrand. It originates in a tract published some twenty years ago by an ex-Anglican theologian who styled himself Dominus — a man once on the path to high preferment, until his anti-Catholic zeal consumed him. I recall reading his writings in an obscure theological review — he had a taste for allegorical inversions of ritual. Dangerous mind. Cold mind."

Brown leaned forward. "Do you recall his name?"

"I do," Holmes said slowly. "He vanished from clerical life under the name of Charles Erskine.

But in certain radical circles, he is now known as Silas Wynter."

I could not help remarking on the chill in Holmes's voice as he pronounced it.

"And you think," I said, "that Wynter has been staging these murders as a form of... anti-mass?"

"Precisely. A calculated inversion of the sacred, designed to outrage the faithful and to lay the blame upon the Irish radicals. An intellectual scheme, Watson — and one far beyond the reach of poor Rourke."

Holmes closed the pamphlet and handed it to Brown. "Guard this well, my young friend. It is the first clear thread that may lead us to the heart of this labyrinth."

Then Holmes did something in all my years with him he had never done. He invited Brown to Baker Street to consult further. I felt that pain again.

Brown leaned forward. "Do you recall his name?"

Chapter VII
The Mind behind the Flame

**he** fog of the East End clung to us as we left St Mary and St Michael's.

Holmes hailed a hansom with an impatient gesture, and the three of us — Holmes, Brown, and I — climbed in. He said little on the rattling ride back to Baker Street, though I could see his mind working like a silent machine. Brown, for his part, clutched a satchel containing the tracts he had discovered, his knuckles white on the strap.

Once home, Holmes cleared the table and spread the pamphlets in neat rows. "Note the script," he said, tapping the printed margins. "This reversed cross here — and here — identical to the one carved into the table beside our dead friar. Rourke's rhetoric is ragged and emotional; these, however, are precise. An educated pen."

Brown nodded. "This one bears the imprint of a printer in Clerkenwell. I've seen it on theological works, and on polemics by an author calling himself Silas Wynter."

"Which is why," Holmes said, "we shall not waste another hour on declaiming radicals. Wynter — real name Charles Erskine — was once considered the most promising Anglican theologian of his generation, until a paper denouncing 'Romish idolatries' cost him his chair. He disappeared into the underworld of anti-Catholic journalism, where his venom found a new audience among Protestant hardliners and political agitators."

Holmes's long finger traced a map pinned to the wall. "Erskine keeps three haunts. One — a print shop in Clerkenwell, where these tracts are likely struck. Two — a boarding house off Stepney Causeway, where he once lectured to temperance societies. Three — a coffee room on Bishopsgate where the editors of *The Protestant Clarion* meet on Thursdays."

Brown leaned forward. "And tomorrow is Thursday."

Holmes's smile was thin. "Just so. We shall pay *The Clarion* a visit, and if Wynter is there, I intend to have a word — though I suspect we will need Lestrade's presence before the night is through."

The next evening, under cover of the usual street noise, we watched from across Bishops-

watched, he drew — not wrote — a reversed cross in the margin.

Holmes turned to us. "Gentlemen, I believe we are looking at the mind behind the flame. And if we are not careful, he will strike again before we can snuff it out."

I believe we are looking at the mind behind the flame.

gate. The coffee room glowed yellow in the fog. Inside, amid the clink of cups, sat a man in a black coat, his high forehead framed by greying hair, his mouth fixed in an expression of permanent disdain. In front of him lay a notebook, and as we

Chapter VIII
Revelation and Confession

**he** plan was simple enough in outline, dangerous in execution.

Lestrade's men would keep watch outside *The Clarion* meeting-room while Holmes, Brown, and I slipped in through the rear entrance of the adjoining church — a disused chapel whose sacristy connected by a narrow door to the coffee room. Holmes reasoned that Wynter, cornered between his audience and his escape, would seek solitude to hide incriminating papers before flight. We would be waiting.

The sacristy was dim, smelling of wax and cold stone. A single candle guttered on the table beside the vestments. Brown moved quietly, checking drawers, until a faint metallic click froze us. The side door opened and Wynter stepped in, closing it behind him. His eyes fell instantly upon Brown.

"You," he said, voice dripping with disdain. "The little catechist. The Vatican's pet ferret."

Brown stiffened, but before he could speak Wynter's hand went to his coat. In a blink a long, slender knife flashed in the candlelight.

"You were at the library. You found the tracts," Wynter said. "That makes you the next idol to topple."

Holmes moved forward, but Wynter shifted to keep Brown between them. "The Irish are too stupid for true revolution," he hissed. "They cling to their Masses and their saints. No — to burn Rome's rot out of England, one must strike the shepherds, one by one, until the flock scatters in fear."

Brown's eyes flicked to a stack of pamphlets on the table. "And you disguise yourself in their cause so they take the blame."

Wynter laughed. "They are tools. Their blood and their tempers stir the pot. But the mind, the design — that is mine."

Holmes's voice was calm but steely. "And the reversed stations of the cross? The anti-masses?"

Wynter's lip curled. "Symbols matter. Inverting theirs shows the void behind their lies. I am giving England a liturgy of truth."

Wynter's answer was a chilling smile. "There will be others. Ideas cannot be hanged."

Lestrade snapped the irons shut.

"You," he said, voice dripping with disdain. "The little catechist."

With a sudden movement, Wynter lunged at Brown. I was halfway across the room when Holmes struck his arm with his cane, the knife clattering to the stones. Lestrade's men burst in from the street side, hauling Wynter back as he spat and shouted curses in both English and Latin.

Holmes bent to pick up the knife, examining the hilt. "A sacrificial blade," he murmured. "And with it, you would have consecrated your final parody."

"We'll see what the Old Bailey thinks of that."

Holmes turned to Brown. "You kept your head admirably, though I suggest next time you allow a little more distance from the point of a blade."

Brown managed a wan smile. "Yes, Mr. Holmes. I'll remember."

Outside, the fog swallowed the shouting as Wynter was led away. The air seemed a fraction lighter, though Holmes's expression was still shadowed. "We have stopped the man," he said, "but the poison he's poured into print will linger."

London's Dockland slums

Chapter IX
A Future in Shadow

**t** was a week after the arrest of Charles Erskine when Holmes and I found ourselves once more in the quiet of Baker Street. Outside, the rain had not ceased since dawn; the steady patter against the panes mingled with the faint hum of the new telephone — an object of some suspicion to Mrs Hudson, though Holmes was already finding it indispensable.

She entered with the post, among which lay a single heavy envelope stamped with the seal of the Vatican. Holmes slit it open with the paper-knife and read aloud:

To Gentile Signor Sherlock Holmes,

The Holy Father extends his gratitude for your service in the matter of the Whitechapel murders. His Holiness commends your dedication to the cause of truth and justice, and prays for the repose of the souls lost. It is his hope that the spirit of concord, of which he has lately written, may take deeper root in England — for the dignity of her workers, the relief of the poor, and the just treatment of her Irish faithful.

In Christo,
Monsignor Paolo,
Private Secretary to His Holiness
Leo PP XIII

"A courteous acknowledgment," he remarked, "but also a reminder, Watson. You may recall His Holiness's recent tract on the working man — *Rerum Novarum*, I believe. Rome calls for fair wages, decent conditions, and the dignity of the poor. A sentiment England might profit from, if she can hear it over the din of her own prejudices."

That same afternoon we took a hansom to St Mary and St Michael's. The rain had eased, and the lamps along the East End streets glimmered through the mist. Brown awaited us on the church steps, the hood of his cloak beaded with water.

"I wished to see you before I leave," he said, shaking Holmes's hand with quiet sincerity. "I return to the seminary tomorrow. My course is nearly complete, and soon I will take Holy Orders."

closed about him. Holmes's gaze lingered on the place where he had vanished. "Mark

"A courteous acknowledgment," he remarked.

Holmes regarded him for a long moment. "Then this will be the last time we meet as Mr Brown. I suspect the world will come to know you as Father Brown — a man with an uncommon eye for truth. Do not let the Church's enemies suppose that only detectives may hunt in the dark."

The young man smiled faintly. "Then I shall hunt in my own fashion, Mr Holmes. The work will be different — the quarry, much the same."

We watched him walk away into the evening crowd until the fog

my words, Watson — the world will hear of him again. And when it does, it will not be for sermons alone."

Editor's Note

The stories contain here are the product of a literary collaboration between myself — a human writer — and OpenAI's ChatGPT. Working within a shared narrative framework, I guided the research, historical detail, and plot development, while the AI provided language, structural clarity, and suggestions in the voice of Dr. Watson and others.

The result, I hope, is true both to the spirit of Conan Doyle and to the possibilities of creative partnership in a new age of storytelling.

Michael Williams, August 2025